$2.50

MYRIAD BOOKS LIMITED
35 Bishopsthorpe Road, London SE26 4PA

First published by
Andersen Press
20 Vauxhall Bridge Road
London SW1V 2SA
www.andersenpress.co.uk

ISBN 1 904 736 84 X

Printed in China

MARINETTA
at the Ballet

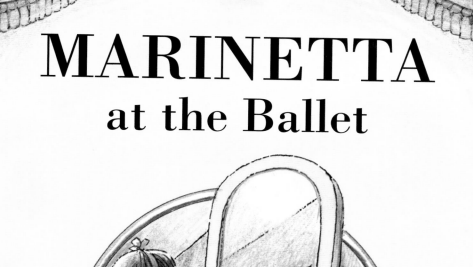

by Elaine Mills

Myriad Books

Marinetta lived in a room of her own
at the top of an old dolls' house.

In the evening after tea she used to dance for
Uncle Theo Bear who played the violin.

One day Uncle Theo bought a set of tickets.
"Come on, everyone!" he said.
"Put on your best clothes – we are going to the ballet!"
Marinetta wore her silver dancing shoes.

When they were all inside the Toy Theatre,
the lights went out.
A beautiful ballerina glided onto the stage.
"Oh!" said Marinetta. "Oh, Uncle Theo, who is that?"
"That's Nina, the prima ballerina," answered Uncle Theo.
"Be quiet now, and watch her dance."

The dancer was dressed in black and white.
She fluttered her arms like the wings of a bird.
She twizzled round and around.
But she never once fell over.

"I wish I could do that," said Marinetta. "I wish I could be
a real ballerina and dance in a ballet with Nina."
"Well," said Uncle Theo, "perhaps, one day, you will."

The next day, he took her to a dancing class.
Marinetta followed the dancing teacher
into a room full of toys.

"One, two, three . . ." said Madame Pizzicato.
"One, two, three, four, five . . ."
All the toys were learning how to dance.

"Try again!" said Madame Pizzicato. "Again and again!"
Marinetta did the best she could.

Day after day she practised every move
in front of a mirror. It was very hard.

But soon she could twizzle round
and around without getting dizzy.

"Well done, my little butterfly!"
said Madame Pizzicato.
"You are going to be a star!"

At last, Marinetta had learnt every step
of her favourite ballet. She was so good that Uncle Theo
bought her another ticket for the Toy Theatre.

Marinetta was very excited.
This time it was the last performance
of the ballet she knew so well.

The curtain went up and Nina, the prima ballerina,
appeared on the stage. Her face was very pale.
"Do you think she's feeling ill?" said Marinetta.
"Hush," said Uncle Theo, "and watch how high she can fly!"
"I love her!" said Marinetta.

The dancer twizzled round and around. She could flutter
her wings like a bird. But why was she dancing so slowly?

All at once, she sank to the floor and the music faded away.
"What is going on?" said Uncle Theo
as the curtain came down.
"I think she must be ill!"
said Marinetta.

A young man came out from behind the curtain.
"I'm so sorry . . ." he told them, "but Nina has a nasty
dose of 'flu. We have to stop the show!"
"Wait a minute!" shouted little Marinetta.
"I think I can help you!"
She leapt up gracefully onto the stage . . .

. . . and disappeared behind the curtain!

When the music began again,
Marinetta was dressed in white.
A thousand sequins sparkled in her hair.
She fluttered across the stage like a tiny bird.
She twizzled round and around.

She danced like a real ballerina.

Uncle Theo Bear was very proud. And at the end,
the audience went wild. They shouted out for more!
The air was full of flowers.

"Atishoo!" said the prima ballerina.
"Darling, that was wonderful!"
She blew her nose.

"Come and see me next week . . .
we MUST dance together."
Marinetta was so happy she could hardly speak.
"You and me, together?" she whispered.
"That has always been my dream!"

So Marinetta's greatest wish came true.
And Uncle Theo played the violin . . .